Santa is coming to Lincoln

Written by Steve Smallman
Illustrated by Robert Dunn and Michael Garton
Designed by Sarah Allen
With special thanks to the Lincoln Visitor Information Centre

First published by HOMETOWN WORLD in 2013
Hometown World Ltd
7 Northumberland Buildings
Bath BA1 2JB

www.hometownworld.co.uk

ISBN 978-1-84993-445-9

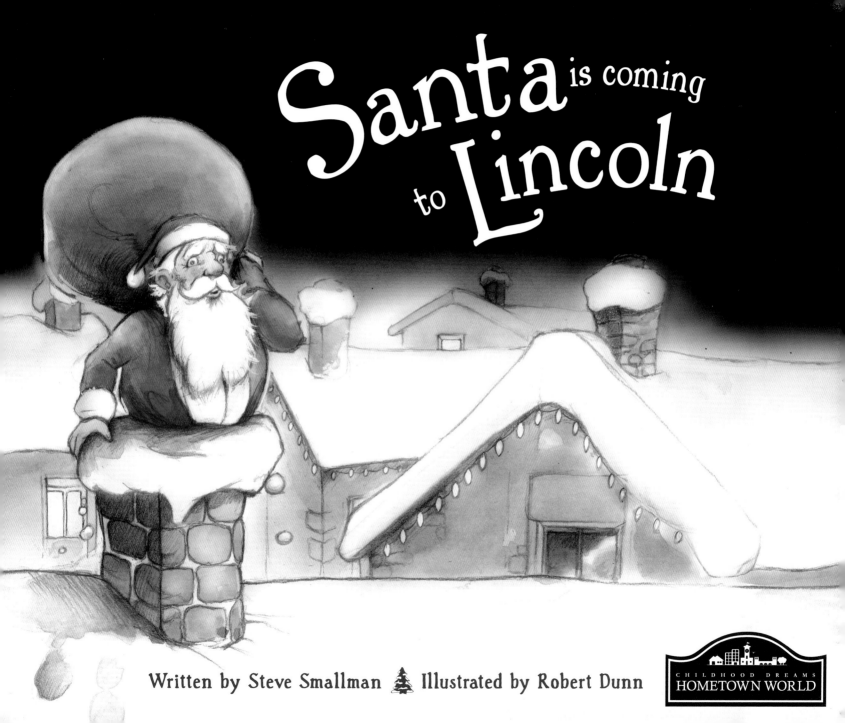

Santa is coming to Lincoln

Written by Steve Smallman 🎄 Illustrated by Robert Dunn

CHILDHOOD DREAMS
HOMETOWN WORLD

"Well?"

boomed Santa. "Have all the children from **Lincoln** been good this year?"

"Well...erm...mostly," answered the little old elf, as he bustled across the busy workshop to Santa's desk.

Santa peered down at the elf from behind the tall, teetering piles of letters that the children of Lincoln had sent him.

"Mostly?" asked Santa, looking over the top of his glasses.

"Yes...but they've all been **especially** good in the last few days!" said the elf.

"Jolly good!" chuckled Santa.
"Then we'd better get their presents loaded up!"

Even though the sack of presents was

really, really big

and the elves were **really, really** small,

they seemed to have no trouble loading it onto Santa's sleigh.
Though how they managed to fit such a big sack onto one little sleigh
even they didn't know. But somehow they did.

"Splendid!" boomed Santa. "We're ready to go!"

"Er...not quite, Santa," said the little old elf. "One of our reindeer is missing!"

"Missing?

Which reindeer is missing?" asked Santa.

"The youngest one, Santa," said the elf. "It's his first flight tonight. I've called him and called him, but..."

Just then, a young reindeer strolled up, munching on a large carrot.

"Where have you been?"

asked Santa.

The youngest reindeer was crunching so loudly that it was no wonder he hadn't heard the little old elf calling.

"Oh well, never mind," said Santa, giving the reindeer a little wink. He took out his Santa-nav and tapped in the postcode for Lincoln. **"This will guide us to Lincoln in no time."**

Crunch!
Crunch!
Crunch!

With a flick of the reins and a jerk of the harness, off they went, racing through the sky.

"Ho-ho-ho!"
laughed Santa.

"We'll soon have these parcels
delivered to the lovely City of Lincoln!"

Santa's sleigh flew through the starry night heading south across the North Sea. On they flew in the crisp, wintry air, crossing the coast over Scarborough. In the wink of an eye, the sleigh was flying above the River Humber and on over Market Rasen. The youngest reindeer was excited. He had never been away from the North Pole before.

They were just crossing over Ellis Windmill
when, suddenly, they ran into a blizzard.
Snowflakes whirled around the sleigh.

They couldn't see a thing!

The youngest reindeer was getting a bit worried,
but Santa didn't seem concerned.

"In two kilometres..."

said the Santa-nav in a bossy lady's voice,

"...keep left at the next star."

"But, Madam," Santa blustered, "I can't see any stars in all this snow!"
Soon they were

hopelessly lost!

Ding-dong!
Ding-dong!

Then, through the howling blizzard, the youngest reindeer heard a faint ringing sound.

Ding-dong!

He looked over at the old reindeer with the red nose. But he had his head down.

(Red nose...I wonder who that could be!)

Ding-dong!
Ding-dong!
Ding-dong!

Ding-dong! Ding-dong!

There was that sound again, like a church bell ringing. The youngest reindeer turned round to look at Santa. But Santa wasn't listening. He seemed to be arguing with a little box with buttons on it.

With a flick of the harness and a jerk of the reins, the youngest reindeer gave a sharp *tug* and headed off towards the sound of the bell, pulling Santa and his sleigh behind him!

"Whoa!"

cried Santa, pulling his hat straight. "What's going on?" Then, to his surprise, he heard a ringing sound.

"Well done, young reindeer!" he shouted cheerfully. "It must be the bell of Great Tom. Don't worry, children, Santa is coming!"

But, suddenly...

CRUNCH!

The sleigh hit something as it plummeted through the snow clouds. **"You have arrived!"** said the Santa-nav unhelpfully.

Finally, when the snow had died down and the clouds parted, Santa discovered exactly where they were...

...stuck, right at the very top of the **Christmas tree** in **Minster Yard!**

"Everybody, PULL!"

The reindeer *pulled* with all their might until, at last, with a screeching noise, the sleigh scraped clear of the Christmas tree. Santa steered them safely over the crooked roofs of Steep Hill, looping around past Brayford Pool, above High Bridge and down into the Arboretum.

Luckily, there
was no real
damage done, but
the parcels had all
been jumbled up. Santa
quickly sorted the presents
into order again.

"Right," said Santa. "Thanks to
this young reindeer I know where
we are now. Don't worry, children,

Santa is coming!"

Santa drove his sleigh expertly from
rooftop to rooftop all over Lincoln, popping in
and out of chimneys as fast as he could go. (Which was
pretty fast
for a chubby
chap!)

There were big chimneys in Skellingthorpe
and small chimneys in Swanpool. He squeezed
down thin chimneys in Birchwood and plummeted
down fat chimneys in Branston.

The youngest reindeer was amazed at how quickly they went. Santa never seemed to get tired at all! And it looked like the children in Lincoln were going to be very lucky this year! But the youngest reindeer was starting to feel a bit weary and quite hungry too.

He piled them under the Christmas
trees and carefully filled up the
stockings with surprises.

In house after house, Santa delved
inside his sack for parcels of every
shape and size.

Santa took a little bite out of each mince pie, a tiny sip of something, wiped his beard and popped the carrots into his sack.

In house after house, the good children of Lincoln had left out a large mince pie, a small glass of something and a big, crunchy carrot.

From Uphill to Downhill, from Ermine to Eagle,
from North Hykeham to Nettleham and ALL
the places in between, Santa and his sleigh
visited every house in Lincoln.

Finally, Santa had delivered the last present
on his long Lincoln list.

"**Great moons and stars!**" sighed
Santa. "It's past midnight and my sack seems as
heavy as ever! I hope I haven't forgotten anyone."

Santa opened his sack to check...but it was full
of juicy, crunchy carrots!

Santa shared out the carrots between all the reindeer.
"Well done, lad!" he said, patting the youngest reindeer gently on the nose.

But the youngest reindeer didn't hear him...he was too busy munching!

Then it was time to set off for home. Santa reset his Santa-nav for
the North Pole and soon they were speeding above Lincoln Castle,
and high past Hartsholme Country Park through the crisp, starry night.